Drained

Joel was sitting on one of the swings, his back to Ted.

"Joel?" Ted called out.

There was no answer.

"Hey, Joel!" Ted said.

But there was still no response from Joel Simmons.

Ted moved toward the swings and gave Joel a friendly smack on the back.

"What the—?" Ted murmured. Joel's body swung slightly. Then his head dropped sharply to one side.

Ted felt his heart begin to race. Joel was unnaturally pale, his skin a sickening bluish white. A thin line of blood trickled from the corner of his mouth, and there were two angry-looking puncture wounds in the side of his neck. His eyes were open, staring up blankly, frozen in eternal shock.

Eve

A novelization by Ellen Steiber
Based on the television series

THE ⓧ FILES™

created by Chris Carter
Based on the teleplay written by
Kenneth Biller and
Chris Brancato

 HarperTrophy®
A Division of HarperCollinsPublishers

To Henri Rozier,
a true X-Phile

Chapter One

The tree-lined streets of Greenwich, Connecticut, blazed with autumn color. The maple leaves were a deep red, the oak leaves golden, and the sky a crisp, clear blue. A whirl of fallen leaves spun by on a cold wind, and Donna Watkins pulled up the collar of her navy blue warm-up suit. She and her husband, Ted, had been jogging for nearly twenty minutes. Usually she'd be sweating by now, but today she just couldn't get warm. Beneath her wool gloves, her fingers were icy. She felt chilled to the bone.

Winter's coming early this year, Donna thought uneasily. Although it was still early in November, many of the trees had already lost their leaves. Their black branches clutched the sky like skeletal fingers. Donna shivered at the sight. She didn't know why, but bare branches always made her think of death.

Donna picked up the pace as they cut across the street and rounded the corner onto their own block. Ted waved at one of their neighbors, Mr. Whelan, who was raking leaves. Mr. Whelan looked perfectly cheerful. Donna tried to shake off her uneasy feeling. After all, it was a beautiful Saturday morning, and she and Ted had recently moved into their dream house. They'd looked for a long time before finding a home in Greenwich. Neither of them wanted to live in one of those suburbs where all the houses were identical and most looked as if they'd been built in an afternoon. Donna loved this neighborhood with its huge trees, wide streets, spacious old homes, and neatly trimmed lawns. There was something reassuring about Greenwich—the sense that everything was in order. Here, things were exactly as they should be.

Donna slowed her pace as she heard a dog

barking in alarm. Later she would remember the dog's bark as the first sign that something was wrong.

She glanced across the street and saw a young girl standing at the end of a circular drive that led to a large, white two-story house. It was Teena Simmons, their neighbor's daughter. She was coatless and shivering, dressed only in a short-sleeved white blouse, pink shorts, and white anklets. She was holding on to a stuffed rabbit.

"What's she doing there by herself?" Donna asked, breathing hard.

Ted shrugged, equally puzzled. Together they crossed the street to find out.

"Teena?" Ted called.

"Honey?" Donna asked, her voice concerned. The eight-year-old girl had seemed quiet when they had met her a few weeks earlier, but this was more than shyness. Although they were standing right next to her, Teena didn't answer. She wouldn't even look at them. She just stood there shivering.

There was something distant in her manner, as if she hadn't heard them. It was the second sign that something was wrong. Seriously wrong.

"You're freezing," Donna said gently. She wondered if the girl was in shock. "Where's your jacket?"

Teena remained silent, hugging her stuffed toy.

"Where's your daddy?" Ted asked.

For the first time, Teena spoke. "In the backyard," she said. "He told me he needed some time to himself."

The couple exchanged puzzled glances.

"I'd say his time's up," Ted said, starting toward the back of the house.

"C'mon, hon," Donna said to the girl. "I'm sure your daddy wouldn't want you to catch cold."

Ted walked around the side of the house to the backyard. He passed a few lawn chairs, a barbecue grill, and a redwood bird feeder. He made his way to the far end of the yard, where Joel Simmons had set up a small playground

4

with swings and a mini-slide.

Joel Simmons was sitting on one of the swings, his back to Ted. He was wearing dark green coveralls.

He was probably doing some yard work and wanted to take a break, Ted figured, not as worried as he'd been a few moments before. "Joel?" he called.

There was no answer.

"Hey, Joel," Ted said, trying to keep it light. "I thought that swing set was supposed to be for your daughter, not you."

But there was still no response from Joel Simmons.

"What the—?" Ted murmured. He moved toward the swings, unaware that Donna and Teena had followed him into the yard.

He gave Joel a friendly smack on the back.

Joel's body swung slightly. Then his head dropped sharply to one side.

Ted felt his heart begin to race. Joel was unnaturally pale, his skin a sickening bluish white. A thin line of blood trickled from the corner of his mouth, and there were two angry-looking puncture wounds in the side of his neck. His eyes were open, staring up blankly, frozen in eternal shock.

Ted jumped as Teena let out an anguished scream. Donna pulled the girl close, shielding her from the sight of her father's grisly corpse.

Stunned, Ted backed away from the body, then began running toward the house. "I'll call 911," he shouted to his wife.

Donna stood by the side of the house, holding on to Teena. The girl was sobbing, her head buried against Donna, her whole body shaking. Donna thought her heart would break when Teena looked toward the swings and whispered, "Daddy."

Donna's world had changed. Minutes earlier Greenwich had felt safe—a place where everything was exactly as it should be. Now that sense of order was gone. And she knew she'd never truly feel safe again.

The winter wind blew, and Joel Simmons's dead body swung like a macabre puppet on the child's swing set.

Chapter Two

In a basement office of the J. Edgar Hoover FBI Building, Special Agent Dana Scully opened a manila envelope and took out a report marked OFFICE OF THE MEDICAL EXAMINER, GREENWICH, CONNECTICUT.

Scully, a young woman with thick reddish blond hair and dark blue eyes, looked somewhat uncomfortable. That was because she always found it difficult to concentrate in her partner's office. Scully couldn't imagine how Fox Mulder found anything—or got any work done—in such a chaotic space. The tiny office was crammed with bulging file cabinets and crowded bookshelves. Every flat surface was covered with thick stacks of magazines, old newspapers, and folders, most of them threatening to topple onto the floor. On one wall was a large poster with the caption "I Want to Believe." What Scully wanted to believe was that someday Mulder would clean up this place. *Not a chance*, she thought, and returned her attention to the file.

" 'Death from hypovolemia,' " she read aloud. " 'Seventy-five percent blood loss.' " She put down the report as she noticed Mulder squinting at a slide. He didn't seem to have heard her.

"That's over four liters of blood," Scully said. "The average healthy adult human only has five and a half liters total." Before joining the FBI, Scully had trained as a doctor and a physicist. She and Mulder made an odd pair. Scully believed in the laws of logic, order, and science. Mulder was willing to believe just about any-thing—the stranger the theory, the better.

"Could say the man was running on empty," Mulder said dryly.

Scully ignored the joke and picked up the report again. The situation was too bizarre to be humorous. She continued briefing Mulder. "The man's daughter—eight years old—was away from his side for no more than ten minutes. She doesn't remember anything. There was no trace evidence to be found at the crime scene."

Mulder moved to a file cabinet. "And any evidence would have been washed away by yesterday's rain," he added, seeming familiar with the case. Despite his casual manner and terrible jokes, Fox William Mulder was one of the agency's finest criminal analysts. Besides being gifted with a photographic memory, he'd studied psychology at Oxford before becoming an FBI agent. Mulder had quickly made a name for himself within the agency by using his knowledge of psychology to create a widely used profile of serial killers. Scully had read his paper and been impressed by how well he understood the criminal mind. Now, though, serial killers were no longer Mulder's focus. He'd chosen another specialty, one that no one else would touch.

"Oh, there were two small puncture wounds in the jugular vein," Scully added.

Mulder opened a file cabinet that was filled

with old, yellowed files. These were his true interest—some might say obsession. These were the X-files, a special set of files begun by J. Edgar Hoover in 1946. The X-files detailed cases that didn't fit within the normal bounds of crime. The files contained reports of such unexplainable events as alien encounters, UFOs, shape-shifters, psychic disturbances—anything that belonged to the realm of the paranormal and supernatural.

Mulder took out several thick X-files and dropped them onto the desk in front of Scully. "Are you at all familiar with the phenomenon of cattle mutilations?"

What could cattle mutilations possibly have to do with a murder in suburban Connecticut? Scully asked herself. Not for the first time, she wondered if her partner was losing it. *Well*, she thought more optimistically, *at least he's not suggesting that vampires did it.*

Mulder turned off the overhead lights. The slide projector clicked on, and pictures of several dead cows on an open range flashed onto the screen.

"Since 1967, over thirty-four states have reported unsolved cases of cattle mutilation," Mulder began.

A second slide, this one of parts of a cow's body, filled the screen. The organs appeared to have been surgically removed.

"The trace evidence is remarkably similar," Mulder went on. "Note the incision marks of surgical precision."

Another slide flashed on. This one showed a close-up of the incision. The cut on the cow was laser sharp, Scully saw.

Mulder stepped behind her, operating the projector by remote and bringing up another slide of the dead cattle.

"There's a substantial degree of blood loss without a trace of blood at the scene," he pointed out.

"How can that be?" Scully asked.

"Exsanguination."

Scully had been partnered with Mulder long enough to know that even if his theories sounded crazy, he was often right. And so she listened, trying to keep an open mind, as he explained something she'd learned long ago in medical school.

"If you were to stick a needle in the jugular of any living creature, the heart itself would act as a pump, pushing all the blood out of the body. Or nearly all of it," Mulder explained. "These animals have had their jugulars punctured in the same way as the man in Greenwich, Connecticut."

He clicked the remote, and a slide of the deceased Joel Simmons appeared on the screen. Scully studied the two angry red puncture wounds on his neck with interest. They certainly didn't look like the bite of any animal she recognized.

Mulder tapped the screen and said, "Only this is the first time I've ever seen it on a human being."

Scully examined the Simmons file again. "But there were no signs of a struggle," she said. "I mean, how could a man just sit through a bloodletting?"

"The medical examiner found traces of digitalis in his remaining blood," Mulder answered. "That's a chemical that can act as a paralytic drug."

"Who would do such a thing?" Scully asked, mentally sorting through the hundreds of cases she'd worked on. "Satanic cults?"

"Cults go for easier prey—children and small animals," Mulder replied. "Something that won't fight back."

"Wait a minute," Scully said, scanning the files Mulder had given her. "These X-files indicate that this is a UFO-related phenomenon. Listen to this: 'Often there are sightings in the sky near the incident . . .'" Scully tried to keep the skepticism out of her voice as she continued, "'. . . surface burns . . .'"

"Witnesses often report time loss," Mulder added. "We've seen this in abduction cases. That might explain why the girl didn't remember anything."

Scully sighed. "Mulder," she said patiently, "why would alien beings travel light-years to Earth to play doctor on cattle?"

"For the same reason we cut up frogs and monkeys," Mulder replied.

Scully looked unconvinced.

"Besides." He went back to the slide of Simmons's neck wound, tapping the screen with the remote. "It appears they may have stepped up their interest."

Scully searched the image on the screen. She was hoping she'd see something in the photograph that would explain the circumstances of Joel Simmons's death. Mulder's UFO theory hadn't persuaded her. Especially because she knew his history. When Mulder was a child, his younger sister had disappeared, kidnapped from her bedroom in the middle of the night. Mulder was convinced that she had been abducted by alien forces while he had been paralyzed by some unknown power that had also altered his memories of the event.

Scully knew enough about his sister's case to admit that it was possible. Still, she couldn't believe that aliens were responsible for the death in Greenwich, Connecticut.

The problem was—she didn't have any better ideas.

Chapter Three

The Fairfield County Social Services Hostel was an old building. In a small room on the top floor, Teena Simmons sat on the edge of a narrow bed, holding tight to her stuffed bunny. The lady who ran the hostel said Teena had the nicest room. She'd made a big deal out of the tall French doors that opened onto a balcony and looked out over the treetops. She kept telling Teena what a great view she had. But Teena didn't care about the view. She didn't like it here. The walls were covered with chipped tan paint. The room was dingy and sparsely furnished—a lumpy bed, a narrow wooden dresser whose drawers all stuck, a rickety desk, and a night table. Everything smelled of disinfectant. It was nothing like her own room at home. Teena missed her bed and her toys. She hugged the bunny tighter. She had a terrible feeling that she might never see her home again.

A cold, light rain was falling when Scully and Mulder reached the Fairfield County Social Services Hostel. The temperature here in Connecticut was at least fifteen degrees cooler than it had been in Washington, and Scully was wishing she'd worn her wool coat instead of the light trench coat. She and Mulder had caught a flight out of D.C. that morning, just hours after being given the Simmons case.

Is this really an X-file? Scully wondered doubtfully as they started up the walk to the hostel. Even if it was, would an eight-year-old girl be able to give them any clue to the cause of her father's mysterious death?

Mulder knocked on the hostel door, taking a quick glance around at the neighborhood. Greenwich was a wealthy community. Teena Simmons had probably lived a privileged life;

he couldn't help wondering what would happen to her now.

A middle-aged woman with a professional yet gentle air opened the door. She wore a blue wool jacket over a blouse and gray wool pants. Her long hair was held back with a barrette, revealing a broad, lined forehead.

Mulder flashed his ID. "Special agents Mulder and Scully."

"You're here about Teena Simmons?" the woman asked.

"Yes," Scully answered. "We'd like to see her, if possible."

The woman held out her hand. "I'm Ms. Wells, the director of the hostel. Please, follow me."

Ms. Wells led them across bare wooden floors to a wooden staircase. Although the building was old, it was clean and well cared for, Scully noted. Everything seemed quiet and orderly. It wasn't nearly as depressing or institutional as other hostels she'd seen.

"Teena's mother passed away from ovarian

cancer two years ago," Ms. Wells explained as she led them up the stairs. "There's no other family. We'll keep Teena here until we can place her with a foster family."

"Has she spoken about it?" Mulder asked as they walked along the well-lit hallway.

"No, not a word," Ms. Wells answered.

"Any nightmares?" Mulder asked.

"No. At least not that I know of." Ms. Wells stopped at a door at the end of the hall. The agents peered through a round window set high in the door.

Teena sat on the edge of a metal-framed bed, clutching a stuffed rabbit. She had long, fine brown hair and straight bangs, wide-set blue eyes, and an upturned nose. She looked younger than Mulder had expected. Young and terribly lonely.

"May we talk with her now?" Scully asked.

"Yes, of course." Ms. Wells knocked and then opened the door.

Teena showed no reaction at all—neither to the sound of the door opening nor to the three people entering the room. *Not a good sign*, Scully thought. The little girl was probably still in shock from her father's death.

"Teena," Ms. Wells said, leaning toward the girl. "These are the people we talked about. This is Ms. Scully and Mr. Mulder. Do you think you can talk to them?"

Teena nodded, her body hunched around the white stuffed rabbit.

As Mulder and Scully approached the bed, Ms. Wells left the room, closing the door behind her.

Scully sat down on the bed beside the girl. Teena looked down, as if concentrating on something on the floor.

"Hi, Teena," Scully began in a soft voice. "I know you must be feeling very sad right now. And scared. But we want to find out what happened so we can catch whoever hurt your daddy. Okay?"

Mulder sat down beside Scully. Teena didn't seem to notice either of them.

"Okay," Scully went on. "Did you ever see any strangers with your daddy at home?"

Teena looked at Scully and shrugged, almost

as if she hadn't understood the question.

Scully hesitated, wondering if she was getting through or if her questions were only upsetting Teena more. She decided to try again. "Did you ever see anyone yell at your daddy or see your daddy yell at someone else?"

"No," Teena said.

"Can you think of anyone who might want to hurt your daddy?" Scully pressed.

Teena thought a moment, then answered, "No."

Mulder spoke up for the first time. "That's a nice bunny, Teena," he said. Teena hugged the rabbit even closer, as if she was afraid Mulder might try to take it away. That kind of fear was to be expected, he thought. After all, both of her parents had been taken away.

"Teena," he said, "can we talk about what happened that day . . . about what happened in the backyard?"

Teena nodded.

"Yeah?" Mulder hesitated for a moment, aware that he was walking on eggshells. The girl seemed to be willing to talk now; he didn't want to say anything that might frighten or discourage her. But there was one thing he was curious about.

"Do you remember any strange sounds . . . or lights . . . or anything like that?" he asked in a soft voice.

Teena looked down for a moment; then her eyes met Mulder's. "There was red lightning . . ."

"Can you tell me more about the red lightning?"

Teena considered, thinking hard. "I can't remember. It . . . all went dark."

"Have you ever seen anything like that before?" Mulder asked, trying not to let his excitement show.

The girl nodded.

"You have? When?"

"The men from the clouds," Teena said clearly. "They were after my dad."

Scully tensed at the girl's words, but Mulder just nodded. As if it was exactly what he'd expected to hear.

Scully's cellular phone rang. She stepped to

the other side of the room before answering it. "Scully," she said.

Then Mulder heard her ask, "Where?" but brought his attention back to the girl on the bed. He was getting close to the case's first real lead—he could feel it.

"Why were these men after your dad?" he asked Teena.

"They wanted to exsanguinate him," she replied matter-of-factly.

Mulder's eyes widened at the girl's casual use of the term. He'd expected a few of Teena's earlier answers. But not this one. Where on earth did an eight-year-old learn a term like that? he wondered.

He had no chance to find out. Scully broke in, her voice urgent. "Mulder," she said.

Mulder crossed the room to his partner, wondering what the problem was.

Scully's face was solemn, her voice hushed as she gave him the news. "There's been another one."

Chapter Four

Shortly after noon the next day, Mulder and Scully drove their rental car across San Francisco's Golden Gate Bridge. Below them, the waters of the bay churned dark blue. Ahead of them were the rounded green hills of Marin County.

Once they were in Marin, Mulder headed for Route 1, the narrow road that wound through the redwoods and above the windswept coastline.

Scully glanced at her map. "We're in earthquake country," she said.

"At least we understand the causes of earthquakes," Mulder said.

This area was very different from New England, he reflected. Northern California was known for mild weather, dramatically beautiful landscapes, and an openness to new ideas and lifestyles. They were three thousand miles away from Connecticut, and yet the white suburban house that was their destination held an uncanny resemblance to the Simmonses' home.

Mulder checked the address on his notepad and pulled up alongside the curb. He and Scully walked through a wooden gate into the backyard. The yard had manicured grass, a redwood bird feeder, a barbecue grill, a swing set, and a small slide.

The two agents surveyed the scene in amazement.

"It's like looking at a mirror image," Mulder said softly.

Scully was not about to get carried away by another one of Mulder's weird theories. Coincidences are often purely random, she reminded herself. She pulled out the case file as they walked toward the swing, determined to stick to the facts.

" 'The victim, Doug Reardon, was married, with one daughter,' " she read aloud. " 'Cause of death: hypovolemia.'" Even Scully couldn't ignore this coincidence. "Mulder, this is uncanny," she admitted. "They also found traces of the poison digitalis in what was left of his blood."

"Puncture wound?" Mulder asked.

"Ah . . ." Scully searched the report. "Yes. On the jugular," she confirmed. "Time of death was estimated at eight thirty A.M. Same day, only three hours earlier than the Simmons murder."

"That's Pacific Standard Time," Mulder reminded her. "Subtract the three-hour difference, and it's the exact same moment."

"It appears we have two serial killers working in tandem," Scully said grimly, closing the folder.

"No," Mulder disagreed. He was pacing the yard, his eyes searching for anything the police might have missed. "Serial killers rarely work in pairs," he said. "And when they do, they kill together, not separately."

"Mulder." Scully tried to keep the impatience out of her voice and failed. "Nothing beyond your leading questions to Teena Simmons substantiates a UFO mutilation theory."

As usual, Mulder was unruffled by his partner's arguments. "Was Reardon's daughter here when he was murdered?" he asked.

Scully checked the report again. "Yes. The police report states that she remembers nothing. Uh, she's with her mother and family in Sacramento right now."

"When will they be back?" Mulder asked.

"Tomorrow."

Mulder looked at his partner. "Even money," he predicted, "she'll remember red lightning."

Thunder rumbled through the skies of Greenwich, and rain poured down in sheets. The clock read 12:35 A.M., but Teena Simmons couldn't sleep. She lay in bed, dressed in flannel pajamas, her arms wrapped around the stuffed rabbit. Her eyes were wide open.

Lightning flashed across the room, and the eight-year-old sat up in bed. She held the rabbit tight, as though that would calm her pounding heart. She could sense something. She didn't know what it was exactly. But it was getting nearer. Second by second. And it was coming for her.

Slowly she lifted off the covers and climbed out of bed, still clutching the stuffed rabbit. Silently she edged toward the door. She peered through the keyhole. The hallway on the other side of the door was completely dark. Ms. Wells had told her that there would always be a light on out there.

Teena's throat tightened. She wondered if the electrical storm had caused a blackout.

Or if something else was responsible.

For a long moment Teena stood by the door, listening.

Suddenly, from the crack at the base of the door, a bright light blasted through.

Teena felt everything inside her go rigid with terror. She had to do something. Fast.

Lightning flared again, and in its light, she searched the room. Her gaze fell on the wooden chair by the desk. Careful not to make a sound, she picked up the chair and leaned it against the door so that the back of the chair jammed the door shut.

She knew she wasn't safe from whatever was coming after her. But at least she had a few seconds now. And maybe that was long enough.

Teena darted toward the French doors which opened onto a rickety wooden terrace. Blinding white lightning flashed as she reached the windows. The storm outside was getting worse. She knew it was dangerous to go outside, but she had no choice. Frantically she pushed against the metal bar that bolted the windows.

It wouldn't budge. Not even an inch. The lock held fast. There was no way out.

And outside her room, someone was turning the knob on the door.

Teena's eyes widened in fright as she watched the door crack open. A beam of bright white light pierced the darkness of the room. The chair she'd propped against the door trembled—but held.

She heard a muffled curse on the other side of the door. And then the chair began to tremble more violently. Whoever was on the other side of the door was suddenly beating against it, trying to break it open.

Panic-stricken, Teena looked around the room for a hiding place.

She dropped to the floor and rolled beneath the bed just as the door of the room burst open. The chair tumbled to the floor with a clatter.

Teena watched, terrified, as the bright beam of light went out. The room was perfectly dark and silent.

Except for a quiet creaking of the floorboards.

Someone was inside with her—slowly crossing the room to the bed.

Thunder crashed through the skies. Lightning lit the room for a split second. And the footsteps drew closer. And closer.

Then, from the other side of the bed, the beam flashed on. Still clutching her beloved rabbit, Teena scuttled out from the opposite side and raced for the open door.

But just as she reached the threshold, powerful hands grabbed her, jerking her backward.

The eight-year-old screamed in synchronicity with a huge clap of thunder. No one would ever hear her over the noise of the storm.

On the ground floor of the hostel a night nurse in a crisp white uniform looked up from her rounds. *What was that sound?* she wondered. *The storm? Or one of the children crying?*

Curious, the nurse started upstairs. She checked on a few of the children and found them sleeping soundly.

Then she walked down the hall that led to Teena's room. Her breath caught as she saw that the door was ajar. Lightning flashed across the floor.

Alarmed, the nurse raced toward Teena's room and pushed the door open the rest of the way.

"Teena?" she cried. "Teena?"

But there was no answer.

Teena's bed was empty. Her desk chair lay

on its side in the middle of the room. The French doors that led to the wooden balcony were flung wide open. Sheets of rain blew into the room, soaking the stuffed rabbit that lay abandoned on the floor.

Chapter Five

Scully and Mulder returned to the Reardon house the following afternoon. The sky was gray, the air damp and cool. As they got out of the rental car and started up the walkway, it wasn't the Reardon murder they were discussing, but Teena Simmons's abduction.

"Teena was kidnapped from the Social Services Hostel around eleven P.M. last night," Scully told Mulder. She'd gotten the call on her cellular phone just moments before. "Looks like someone was afraid she might remember too much."

"Someone . . . or some*thing,* Scully."

That, Scully thought, was exactly why other agents referred to Mulder as "Spooky." His list of suspects usually included beings in both the known and the *unknown* universe.

Scully, however, believed in sticking to the facts.

"Connecticut state troopers set up roadblocks within half an hour of her disappearance," she reported. "Nothing."

"Maybe they weren't looking in the right direction," Mulder said, smiling and nodding toward the sky. Sometimes he couldn't resist teasing Scully; she took everything so seriously.

Scully sighed as Mulder lifted the metal knocker and tapped out a rhythm on the Reardons' front door. Did he really believe this whole case was the work of aliens? Scully considered that theory highly unlikely. It was an unusual double murder—that, she'd admit. But there was nothing supernatural about either killing.

On the other side of the door, Scully heard footsteps. Clearly, this wasn't the time to argue with her partner. Ignoring his last comment, she wrapped up the conversation. "Well, I told the Connecticut police to contact us in case they find her."

The door opened, and Scully and Mulder's expressions turned to astonishment.

A little girl stood in the doorway. She was wearing a brightly striped polo shirt and jeans. And she was eerily familiar. Long brown hair, straight bangs, wide-set blue eyes, and a small, upturned nose. She was the exact image of Teena Simmons.

"Teena?" Scully asked in disbelief.

"No," the girl said.

"Wh-What's your name?" Scully asked.

"Cindy Reardon."

"You live here, Cindy?" Mulder asked.

"Ever since I was born. Eight years ago," the girl announced innocently.

Twenty minutes later, inside the homey living room of the Reardon house, cartoon characters chased each other across the TV screen. Cindy sat on the floor in front of the TV, her expression one of boredom.

Mulder and Scully stood nearby as Cindy took the remote and changed the channel to C-Span. Then the girl settled back, apparently content to view the president introducing a bill to Congress.

Mulder watched the little girl in disbelief. Cindy Reardon was definitely the first eight-year-old he'd come across with an interest in foreign policy.

He glanced around the rest of the house, taking mental notes. If he had to find one word to describe the Reardon home, it would be *cozy*. Dried herbs hung from the ceiling, and the kitchen walls were covered with a bright, flowered wallpaper. A large, colorful handmade quilt hung above the stairway to the second floor. The colors in the house were warm and inviting, the furniture comfortable. It was obvious that a happy family lived here.

Ellen Reardon took three mugs from a cabinet and set them on the counter. Her movements methodical, she began to brew a pot of tea. She was a middle-aged woman with straight, reddish shoulder-length hair and sharp, intelligent eyes. Her face was drawn, though, worn beyond her years. It was a look Mulder had seen too many times, the look of someone who was grieving. It had only been a few days since her husband died.

"Cindy really is a beautiful girl," Mulder said as Mrs. Reardon offered him a steaming mug of tea.

"Doug and I wanted to spoil her," Mrs. Reardon said wistfully. "We wanted to protect her from everything horrible in the world." Starting to cry, Mrs. Reardon choked out her next words. "Cindy was Daddy's little girl."

"Is she an only child?" Mulder asked.

Mrs. Reardon nodded. Her eyes focused on a photograph on the fireplace mantel, a photo of Cindy and her dad.

Scully had a good idea of what her partner was getting at. She cleared her throat and said, "May I ask, was Cindy adopted?"

"No," Mrs. Reardon said, looking offended. "I gave birth to her. At San Rafael General."

Scully knew her next few questions would upset the woman, but she also knew she had to ask them. The resemblance between the girls was too strong to be overlooked; they *had* to be twins. "So," Scully said, "I assume you have all the proper documentation. The birth certificates . . ."

"Of course I do," Mrs. Reardon said. It was obvious that she was confused by Scully's line of questioning.

"Was she the only child delivered at that birth?" Mulder asked.

Ellen Reardon turned to him, shocked. "What the hell kind of question is that? Look, I have told the police everything I know . . ."

Mulder produced a snapshot from his pocket and handed it to Cindy's mother. "Mrs. Reardon, have you ever seen this man before?"

Mrs. Reardon studied the photograph, bewildered. It was a picture of her daughter, wearing a strange purple jacket and sitting on the shoulders of a fair-haired man she'd never seen before. She looked at the agents fearfully.

"Is this man . . . your suspect? Did he . . . do something to Cindy?"

Scully stepped forward at once, wanting to calm the woman. "No," she said firmly. She pointed to the girl in the photograph. "Mrs. Reardon, this is not your daughter."

"I—I don't underst . . ." Mrs. Reardon was shaking her head, unable to believe what she saw, terrified of what it might mean.

"That girl's name is Teena Simmons," Scully went on.

Just a few feet away, Cindy stared at the television screen. But she wasn't really paying much attention to the show. Although her back was turned to the agents and her mother, she was listening intently to their every word.

"This girl—Teena Simmons—lives three thousand miles away in Greenwich, Connecticut," Scully explained.

"That man, her father, was killed in the same manner as your husband," Mulder added.

"Cindy is *my* daughter," Mrs. Reardon said, as if it was the one thing in the world she was still sure of. "I can show you videos of her birth . . . we tried for six years to become pregnant . . ."

Mulder cut her off, his interest piqued. "In vitro fertilization?"

She nodded.

That added a fascinating dimension to the case, Mulder thought. And perhaps the beginning of an explanation of how Teena and Cindy could look so much alike. *In vitro* meant *within an artificial environment*, such as a test tube. Normally the father's sperm fertilized the mother's egg inside her womb. In vitro fertilization meant that with the help of technology, Mrs. Reardon's egg had been fertilized outside her body and then implanted in her womb.

"At which clinic?" Mulder asked.

"The Luther Stapes Center, down in San Francisco."

Scully took careful note of the answer.

And so did Cindy.

Chapter Six

Scully's mind was racing as she followed Mulder out of the Reardon home. She felt as if she had a handful of pieces belonging to a jigsaw puzzle—and she had no idea where the rest of the pieces were, or what they might look like if she could put them together.

There was one piece, however, that didn't fit at all. "Do you still believe this is UFO related?" she asked Mulder as they approached their rental car. "Cindy Reardon didn't see red lightning," she reminded him.

"I don't know," Mulder admitted. "The only thing similar about these girls *does* seem to be their appearance."

"Well, there is a random probability that two people can have an unrelated likeness," Scully said.

"Who both just *happen* to see their fathers exsanguinated?" Mulder asked skeptically. "I'd like to get the odds on that in Vegas."

Scully knew he had a point, but she wasn't about to give him the satisfaction of telling him so.

"You must have studied genetics in medical school," Mulder said as they got into the car. "How do you account for such identical kids coming from two different sets of parents?"

"It's certainly not common," Scully said. She thought about the question, trying to picture a scenario that would account for the coincidence. Genetics, the branch of science that studied the mechanism of heredity, was extremely complex.

"Genetics wasn't my specialty," she admitted, "but the basics work something like this. The characteristics we inherit from our parents are determined on a microscopic level within the cells of our bodies. Chromosomes, which carry that genetic information, are made of a chemical called DNA. Every human being has forty-six chromosomes, made up of twenty-three pairs. One set of each pair comes from the father, the other set from the mother. You get the full set of forty-six when the father's sperm fertilizes the mother's egg. For every inherited trait, a gene from the mother interacts with one from the father. It's why every human being is unique. No two of us are alike—except twins, and you can only get identical twins when they're born from the same egg."

Mulder pulled away from the curb. "That means that Cindy and Teena, who had two completely different sets of parents, should have had very different sets of chromosomes—and very different characteristics."

"Exactly," Scully said. "The coincidences don't make sense. At least not with the information we have so far."

"And nothing so far explains the other similarities: the crime scenes, the way their fathers—" Mulder broke off to check his rearview mirror. He glanced into it again and saw only a quiet suburban street behind them. There was no hint that a man had been murdered there earlier that week.

"The girls are the one and only link between the identical murders," Scully said in a troubled voice.

Mulder turned a corner. The Reardon house was now out of view.

"And one girl was just abducted," he reminded Scully.

"Kidnapped," Scully corrected him.

" 'You say po-*tay*-to, I say po-*tah*-to . . .' " Mulder sang softly, teasing her with the old song.

About a block from the Reardon house, he pulled over and parked the car.

"What are you doing?" Scully asked, puzzled.

"If the murders were committed by the same person or persons, and part of the pattern involves kidnapping the daughter . . ."

"Then you'd expect the pattern to continue," Scully said, finishing his thought.

Mulder nodded. "I'm going to keep an eye on the girl. You check out the clinic. See if the Simmonses were enrolled in the same fertility program."

"Okay," Scully agreed. "I'll call the San Francisco bureau and get some backup to relieve you."

Mulder got out of the car. Carefully he moved into a position where he could stake out the Reardon house. He settled into his post as Scully drove toward San Francisco.

Who was coming for Cindy Reardon? he wondered. *And why did they want her?*

Chapter Seven

Scully drove back across the Golden Gate Bridge, then patiently maneuvered through San Francisco's busy weekday traffic. Her eyes widened as she drove up a hill so steep that it was nearly vertical. For a few seconds she wondered if the rental car would make it. She breathed a sigh of relief as she reached the top, then headed down the other side, past elegant Victorian houses, toward the business district. There was no other city like San Francisco, she thought. Beautiful, exciting, unpredictable—and a natural magnet for some of the stranger incidents in America's history.

A short distance past the TransAmerica pyramid, Scully found what she was looking for: a downtown office building whose sign

read LUTHER STAPES CENTER FOR REPRODUC-
TIVE MEDICINE.

Scully had called ahead and made an appointment with a Dr. M. Bennett, the director of the Stapes Center. Still, she was surprised when she gave her name to the lobby security guard and Dr. Bennett himself came down to escort her through the clinic.

Bennett was a tall, distinguished-looking man with gray hair and a gray mustache. Though he seemed to be in his early sixties, he walked at a brisk pace as he led Scully down a series of sparkling-clean corridors toward his office. Scully studied him carefully, measuring him against the doctors she'd worked with during her medical training. *No immediate red flags*, she decided. Everything about the man radiated responsibility, efficiency, and competence.

"In vitro fertilization is a procedure in which, with a couple's raw material—the eggs and sperm—we can implement fertilization and then implant the embryo into the uterus,"

Bennett explained. "It's helped many couples who couldn't have children on their own."

Scully didn't tell him that she was a doctor and already knew all that. She wanted to give him a chance to talk, to see what he would tell her.

"Could a patient believe she was receiving her own egg but actually receive another without her knowledge?" Scully asked.

"Not here," Dr. Bennett assured her. "We have very strict controls."

"Are you aware of ever having patients by the name of Claudia and Joel Simmons?"

"Any information on our patients is kept confidential," Bennett replied crisply. "It's our policy."

That is exactly what a good doctor should answer, Scully thought. All doctors were obligated to protect their patients' right to privacy. But there were certain circumstances that outweighed that right.

"Both the Simmonses are dead, and their daughter has been kidnapped," Scully informed Bennett. "I'd say any information you have that can help our investigation would override your policy."

Dr. Bennett nodded briefly, indicating that he would cooperate.

Scully followed the clinic director into a spacious office overlooking the bay. *The Stapes Center must do very well,* Scully thought. Bennett had what was clearly an expensive oil painting on the wall behind his desk, and the office was sparingly but beautifully decorated with comfortable leather chairs, a fine oak desk, and the kind of large, exotic plants that require special gardeners to maintain them. Even more impressive were the huge windows that looked out on the bay. San Francisco had some of the priciest real estate in the world, Scully knew. No one here could afford offices like this unless they had an extremely profitable business.

Bennett spoke to his secretary through the intercom. Moments later he handed Scully a manila folder with a red tab labeled SIMMONS, C & J.

Scully opened the folder and began to look

through the file, aware that Dr. Bennett was watching her with concern.

"You had copies of the Simmons' records transferred to Greenwich, Connecticut, in 1991 . . ." she noted. She kept reading, looking for something that might connect Teena Simmons and Cindy Reardon. "The Simmonses came here nine years ago, under the supervision of a Dr. Sally Kendrick."

At the mention of Kendrick's name, Dr. Bennett lowered his head. He shut his eyes as if it was something he didn't want to remember.

"Is there a problem?" Scully asked, noticing his reaction.

"Dr. Kendrick . . . was nothing *but* a problem," Bennett told her. "There's something I should show you," he added. He stood and walked over to the television in his office.

The videotape began with modern-looking graphics and a title that read "An Educational Video for the Luther Stapes Center for Reproductive Medicine." This was followed by even bolder letters, announcing that the topic of the tape was in vitro fertilization.

The graphics faded, giving way to a tall, attractive woman wearing a white medical jacket over a tweed skirt. Dark, straight chin-length hair framed a long, oval face with deep creases along the sides of the mouth.

"Hello, and welcome to the Luther Stapes Center for Reproductive Medicine," the woman began in a friendly voice. "I'm Dr. Sally Kendrick, a specialist in the exciting field of in vitro fertilization . . ."

Dr. Bennett paused the video and glanced at Scully. "Kendrick was a resident here in 1985," he explained. "Brilliant scientist. First in her class at Yale Med, where she got her M.D. after completing her doctorate in bio-genetics. We were thrilled to get her."

Bennett walked back to his desk and sat down heavily in his chair.

"And now you don't sound so thrilled," Scully observed.

"We have reason to believe Dr. Kendrick

was tampering with the genetic material of fertilized ova in the lab prior to implant. Experimenting with the study of eugenics—hereditary improvement by genetic control."

"Did you report this to the American Medical Association?" Scully asked, knowing how serious a charge it was.

"Of course," Dr. Bennett replied. "And I fired her. I also requested an investigation from the U.S. Department of Health and Human Services."

"And what happened?"

"The A.M.A. censured her, but my request for an investigation was denied. As for Dr. Kendrick . . . she just disappeared."

Bennett hit the Play button on the remote control, and Sally Kendrick, now sitting at her desk, continued her pitch.

"We at the Stapes Center understand the pain of infertility, and we are ready to help. In the next half hour, I'll guide you through the IVF program, from consultation to fertilization. You'll also hear from some patients who have completed the cycle and delivered a healthy baby . . ."

Scully sat riveted by the video. She already knew the information on in vitro fertilization. It was Sally Kendrick who fascinated her. Kendrick was an eloquent speaker, capable of distilling complex scientific concepts into easily understood language. She was also warm and charming, the kind of doctor anyone would trust.

But Scully recognized something in her that she'd seen before, in other cases. Although Kendrick's voice had the right intonation and her face all the right expressions, she had what Scully thought of as the fever. This had nothing to do with body temperature. It was instead a manic glitter that you often saw in the eyes of people who were on the edge. They might appear perfectly normal to the outside world and even very successful, but inside they were teetering on the brink of a major emotional meltdown. Scully concentrated on Kendrick as she continued speaking. No, Scully wasn't imagining it. It was definitely there. Kendrick had that look, Scully thought, exactly the kind of look she'd seen time and again in the eyes of people who killed.

Chapter Eight

In a San Francisco motel room that evening, Scully showed Mulder the video Dr. Bennett had shown her that afternoon. Mulder watched intently, Sally Kendrick's image reflected in his glasses.

"Kendrick was the supervising physician in both the Simmonses' *and* the Reardons' IVF program," Scully explained. "It seems she was experimenting at the clinic. Bennett believes she was tampering with the eggs of the women who came to the clinic for help—possibly trying to change the genetic makeup of their DNA."

"And maybe now she's trying to erase the results," Mulder speculated.

On the TV screen, Sally Kendrick ended her presentation with a smile and an encouraging tone. "I wish we could guarantee everyone success, but with our scientific advances, a little luck, and a lot of hope, miracles *can* happen."

Mulder turned off the VCR and stared at the blank screen as if at a loss for words. Scully knew he'd recognized that look burning in Kendrick's eyes.

"Well, she must have an accomplice in order to have done both murders," Scully said.

"So do you think this is some vendetta she and a colleague have against the Stapes Center?" Mulder wondered aloud.

The phone rang, and Scully got up to answer it. "Mulder," she said before picking up the receiver, "does this mean you've finally abandoned your UFO theory?" The phone rang again. Scully picked it up. "Hello," she said. "Hello . . ."

On the other end of the line, someone hung up.

Scully put down the receiver and shrugged. "Just a few clicks. Must be a wrong number."

Mulder stood up, took off his wire-rimmed

glasses, and rubbed the bridge of his nose. "I'll tell you what," he said. "I'm going to sleep on it, and we'll talk about it in the morning." He began to walk her to the door.

"Mulder, you're rushing me out of the room," Scully protested, puzzled. Moments before, he'd wanted to discuss the case. Now he wanted her to leave.

"No, I'm not," Mulder insisted, putting a hand on her shoulder and escorting her to the door.

Scully's voice became teasing. "Do you have a girl coming over?"

"What's a girl?" Mulder joked. "I've got a movie I want to watch on TV. Sleep tight. I'll see you in the morning."

He shut the door and glanced at the phone. When he heard Scully's door close farther down the corridor, he pulled on a jacket and quietly slipped outside.

It was nearly midnight, and the marina was quiet. Boats bobbed gently against the docks.

The red and white lights strung along the pier reflected in the dark water of the bay.

Cautiously Mulder stepped out from behind one of the boathouses. He looked around, his eyes searching the shadows. His body tensed as he saw something move—and relaxed as he realized it was only a cat. He headed toward the water, walking casually, as if he were just out for an evening stroll.

Then, from somewhere in the darkness, he heard a familiar voice. "Are you certain she hasn't followed you?"

Mulder stepped toward the voice and nodded. "What are you doing here?" he asked.

Deep Throat emerged from behind a stand of trees and stepped halfway into the light. He was a middle-aged man with a receding hairline and deep shadows beneath his eyes. "I thought we could take in a Warriors game."

Mulder smiled at the joke—and at the idea of attending a basketball game with the mysterious informant—but he was wondering if Deep Throat was going to warn him off the case. More than once Deep Throat had advised Mulder that he was going into areas better left untouched. And he had been right every time.

Mulder had never really figured out who Deep Throat was or how he got his information. Deep Throat hinted that he'd once worked for the CIA and that he now belonged to an organization that was responsible for "heinous acts against man." Sometimes Mulder thought Deep Throat could be using him and Scully—using them to try to bring down whoever it was he worked for. All Mulder knew for certain was that the man had access to some of the U.S. government's most highly classified top secret documents. And for reasons Deep Throat would never reveal, he occasionally chose to share those secrets with Mulder.

"Actually," Deep Throat said, "I was . . . just in the neighborhood and wondered if I had ever told you about the Litchfield experiments."

Mulder shelled a sunflower seed and played along, knowing it was best not to ask Deep Throat too many direct questions. "Hmmm . . . no, you haven't."

"Well, it was a most interesting project," Deep Throat said. "Highest level of classification. All records have since been destroyed. And those who knew of it will deny knowledge of its existence."

Mulder listened, both intrigued and wary. Deep Throat had helped him more times than he could count. He had also lied to him once. Deep Throat was worth listening to, but he was not someone Mulder would ever really trust.

"In the early fifties," Deep Throat went on, "during the height of the Cold War, we got wind that the Russians were fooling around with eugenics, the study of improving human genetics through science. Rather primitively, I might add—trying to crossbreed their top scientists, athletes, you name it, in order to come up with the superior soldier." He waited a beat, then added in a dry tone, "Naturally, we jumped on the bandwagon . . ."

Mulder immediately saw the connection to his case. "These Litchfield experiments . . ."

Deep Throat nodded. "A number of genetically controlled children were raised and monitored on a compound in Litchfield. The boys were all called Adam, and the girls were all called Eve."

"Quaint," Mulder observed. But his brain was already making rapid calculations. These children would be in their forties now.

"They were numbered to distinguish one from the other," Deep Throat explained.

Which meant, Mulder guessed, that the children had been difficult to tell apart. In fact, it was possible that all the girls were genetically identical, and all the boys as well. "Whatever happened to the Adams and the Eves?" Mulder asked.

Deep Throat pursed his lips, tense. "There's

a woman you should see. I'll make sure you can get in."

"Where?"

"In a tiny corner in the basement of the Whiting Institute."

"Who is she?" Mulder asked.

"Eve Six," Deep Throat answered, and once again disappeared into the shadows.

Chapter Nine

Late the next afternoon Mulder and Scully entered the small town of Litchfield, California. Litchfield, they'd discovered, was nearly four hundred miles northeast of San Francisco, a town so remote that there were no airports nearby. They'd spent the entire day in the car, and now they were almost at the Nevada border.

"What do you know about eugenics, Scully?" Mulder asked.

Scully, who was driving, never took her eyes off the road. "It's one of those topics that causes a lot of debate in medical ethics classes," she replied. "We now have the ability to make some changes to the human genetic pattern. The question is, should we?"

"Well?" Mulder asked.

Scully sighed as the road curved and the high cinder-block wall surrounding the Whiting Institute came into view.

"From a scientific standpoint eugenics is very intriguing," she said. "For example, diseases like cystic fibrosis are inherited, untreatable, and always fatal. With gene therapy we might be able to alter the DNA and wipe out the disease completely."

"But?" Mulder asked, sensing an unspoken objection in her voice.

"But there's always a danger of using that kind of genetic manipulation for political or social agendas," Scully said. "In the nineteenth century a man named Francis Galton founded a eugenics movement whose goal was the controlled improvement of the human race by selective breeding. Galton was convinced that geniuses ran in families and were the result of superior heredity. So he tried to encourage people with 'the best qualities' to mate with each other."

"Sounds like what the Russians wanted to do in the fifties," Mulder said.

"Neither Galton nor the Russians understood enough about genetics to succeed," Scully said. "But in the 1920s a number of our universities and government leaders backed the eugenics movement. The result was that they sterilized 58,000 people whom they considered genetically inferior—criminals, the mentally retarded, people with epilepsy . . ."

"The creation of a 'master race.' Hitler would have loved it," Mulder said.

Scully turned down the long drive that led to the institute. "That's the problem. I think most people would agree that certain physical conditions—like cystic fibrosis, or even obesity—are undesirable. We'd get rid of them if we could. But if you take that ability one step further, then what else do you get rid of? People who are *almost* obese? Overweight? Mildly overweight?"

Mulder nodded. "Who decides what's desirable and undesirable? The danger is, the one who decides could be someone like Hitler."

"There's another danger," Scully said as she pulled up alongside the institute's outer gate. "Our knowledge of genetics is still relatively unsophisticated. A scientist might have the best intentions. But there's always the risk that when you play with DNA—or play God, as some people say—you're going to make a very serious mistake."

Having parked and passed through three outer gates, Mulder and Scully moved toward a guard in a glassed-in booth in Whiting's Cellblock Z.

"Mulder," Scully asked uneasily, "who told you about this place?"

"I wish I knew who he was," Mulder said honestly.

"Is this your 'inside' friend?" Scully pressed.

"*Friend* is perhaps too strong a word," Mulder replied. He was still wary of the mysterious informant. An informant always sold *someone* out, and there were no guarantees that Mulder wasn't the one being betrayed. Mulder had made plenty of enemies since joining the FBI. What if Deep Throat worked for one of them and was setting him up?

The two agents approached the guard's desk and presented their credentials.

"FBI agents Mulder and Scully to see . . . Eve Six," Mulder said.

"Deposit your firearms and sign for these," the guard said in a bored monotone as he dropped two alarm beepers onto the desk.

"What are these?" Mulder asked.

"Panic buttons," the guard explained. "Wouldn't let you go in without one."

A female guard unlocked the heavy steel door that led into the wards. She slid it shut behind them with a clang. The two agents followed her inside a tower that was lined with endless rows of prison cells, one stacked on top of another. Inmates jeered and screamed at them from behind bars. The noise was deafening.

The guard led them down a steep flight of stairs to a basement corridor. Mulder had the feeling that this area had never known daylight or even warmth. It was damp and cold here, and the six doors that lined the hall gave no hint of what they contained.

Another guard stepped forward, unlocked another steel door, and joined the first to lead them to a cell marked EVE 6. Its door had only a narrow slit of a window, with steel wire sandwiched between the layers of glass. *Whoever Eve Six is, she certainly requires serious security,* Scully thought.

Together the two guards opened the lock on the cell door. Wordlessly the second guard handed Scully a flashlight. "Why the flashlight?" Scully asked.

"She screams and screams if we turn on the overheads," the guard explained, not unsympathetically. "No one's ever got a real good look at her." She paused, then said, "We'll be right outside."

Scully opened the cell door. The interior of the cell was pitch black.

"Hello," Mulder said as Scully guided the flashlight beam about the tiny room with padded walls.

The light moved over the cold gray cement floor to an empty chair, to the end of a thin, bare mattress covered in striped ticking.

Scully's light stopped on red ankle restraints attached to the concrete wall. She shined the light upward—from the red cuffs to the legs wrapped in loose green institutional pajamas. The prisoner sat chained on a metal cot that was attached to the wall. Her arms were bound in front of her by a white straitjacket. She blinked in the harsh light.

Mulder and Scully stood silently, neither quite believing what they saw.

It was Eve Six who spoke first, her voice bitter. "So . . . I guess you've found what you're looking for." She looked at them directly. "One of us, at least."

Scully shined the light on the woman's face. Eve Six squinted, looked down, tried to escape the light. Normally Scully would have felt sorry for her and moved the light at once. But she was too stunned to do anything but stare. It couldn't be. This woman had short, greasy, unkempt hair, the ends jagged, as if someone had chopped it off with a knife. Her yellowed teeth were rotting, and her eyes were sunken and psychotic. Her gaze burned with a fierce, frightening intensity.

Still, Scully knew she was looking at the same woman she'd seen in Dr. Bennett's videotape.

"Sally Kendrick," Scully said at last.

Chapter Ten

Eve Six leaned back against the corner of the bed, her knees drawn up to her chest. Her eyes were red-rimmed as if she'd been crying. "Unlock the chains," she said in a calm voice. "Then we'll talk."

"They're probably there for a good reason," Mulder said cautiously.

"No," Eve contradicted him. "Bad reason. I paid too much attention to a guard. Bit into his eyeball." She bared her decaying, yellowed teeth, gnashing them together with a high, nervous laugh.

Receiving no reaction from the agents, she shrugged and offered a point of clarification. "I meant it as a sign of affection," she said.

Mulder knew she was trying to scare them, and he had no intention of letting her succeed. He stared at her, waiting for her to drop the act.

His silence seemed to make her nervous. "Are you here to give me an IQ test, by any chance?" she asked, speaking rapidly. "I think I can top 265. We're very bright, we Eves. It runs in the family."

Mulder weighed her claims against what he knew from his training as a psychologist. A person of average intelligence would have an IQ score somewhere between 90 and 110. Ninety-five percent of everyone tested fell somewhere between 70 and 130. An IQ of 140 was usually considered genius level. 265? It was simply off the charts.

"Where are the rest?" he asked. "The Adams and the other Eves?"

"We're prone to suicide," Eve Six said softly. "I'm the only one left here. Eve Seven escaped early on. And Eve Eight. She escaped ten years later."

"Are you Sally Kendrick?" Scully asked.

"That's not my name," the woman told them, staring off into the darkness at something only she could see. "But she is me . . . and I am her. 'And we are all together.' " She sang the last words in a flat, tuneless voice, a parody of an old Beatles song.

"Did you work for the Luther Stapes Center for Reproductive Medicine in 1985?" Scully asked, getting back to the facts.

"In 1985?" Eve Six echoed furiously. "By 1985 I had been tied up like this for two years." She struggled in the straitjacket, futilely trying to lift her arms. "And for what reason? *No reason.* I did nothing. I'm just me. They *made* me. But do they suffer? No, no. *I* suffer. I *suffer.* They keep me alive for the Litchfield project. They come in, they poke me, they test me to see what went wrong." Eve's pained voice became sly with calculation. "Sally knows what went wrong."

Mulder eyed Scully, wondering how much of what Eve Six said could be believed. Even if her claims about her IQ were outrageous, he had an awful feeling that most of what she said was true. The Eves couldn't help what they were. They *had* been made, the result of a government experiment—and now this woman was doomed to a lifetime of imprisonment because of it.

"You and you. You have forty-six chromosomes in twenty-three pairs," Eve Six said, sounding curiously like a biology teacher. "The Adams, me, the other Eves, we have fifty-six. We have extra chromosomes, numbers four, five, twelve, sixteen, and twenty-two. This replication of chromosomes also produces additional genes. Heightened strength. Heightened intelligence."

"Heightened psychosis," Mulder added.

Eve Six flashed him the ghost of a smile. "Saved the best for last."

She stared at Scully. "You don't believe me," she said, sensing her doubts. "I have proof. Look on the wall." She raised one foot the short distance the restraints allowed, pointing upward. "My family album."

Scully moved to the wall with her flashlight. Newspaper clippings and eerie drawings were taped to the cement wall. Finally Scully found a photo of eight little girls, all dressed in school uniforms. The length and cut of their plaid skirts told her that the picture had been taken in the 1950s. The Eves were gathered in a schoolyard, some on the swings, others posed by a tree. The girls were smiling at the camera, every one of them identical.

And every one of them a dead ringer for Teena and Cindy.

"My God," Scully whispered. "It's the girls."

"We were close," Eve Six said whimsically. "We were *very* close."

"Sally Kendrick was using the clinic to continue the Litchfield experiment," Mulder said. He stared at the wreck of a woman that was Eve Six, suddenly understanding. "She was cloning herself."

Chapter Eleven

Night had fallen, blanketing the green hills of Marin County in darkness. In a cheerful bedroom decorated with striped pastel wallpaper and pictures of angels, Cindy Reardon knelt beside her bed and said her prayers. Her mother stood in the doorway, watching.

"'Now I lay me down to sleep,'" the eight-year-old began. "'I pray the Lord my soul to keep. If I should die before I wake, I pray the Lord my soul to take.' God bless Grandma and Grandpa Stenner, Irma and Irmapop. And God bless Mom. And please take care of Daddy up in heaven."

As Cindy finished her prayers, Mrs. Reardon came to sit on the bed beside her. Blinking back tears, she stroked her daughter's hair. "You're such a special little girl, Cindy," she said.

She tucked her daughter under the covers and kissed her on the forehead. "Good night, honey," she said.

Although Ellen Reardon had known Cindy since the day she was born, she had no real idea of just how special she was.

Outside the Reardon house, Mulder and Scully sat in the rental car and watched as the light in Cindy's room winked out. They had just replaced the agents who had been watching the house all day.

The relief agents had reported little or no activity at the Rearden home. But the peaceful scene did nothing to reassure Mulder. He couldn't shake the vision of Eve Six, chained to the wall, crazed and pathetic and frightening.

"If Eve Six is right, and there are two other Eves out there," Mulder said, "that could account for the two identical murders occurring at exactly the same time. Sally Kendrick does have an accomplice: herself."

Scully leaned her elbow against the door and rested her head on her hand. "Until I heard that . . . I was beginning to suspect the girls."

"No," Mulder said. "It seems the two remaining Eves are doing away with the parents in order to keep Teena and Cindy in the family."

"Do you suppose the girls have any idea of what they really are?" Scully asked, raising binoculars to study Cindy's window.

"I hope not," Mulder replied.

Cindy closed her eyes and waited. She listened as she heard her mother softly shut her bedroom door and then go back downstairs.

Careful not to make a sound, Cindy sat up in bed. Someone was in the house. Someone who didn't belong there.

Swallowing hard, Cindy checked under the bed. There was nothing there. Hugging her favorite stuffed animal to her chest, she got up and moved to the window, locking it. Then she stood by the window, staring out over the darkened street.

Down below, Mulder and Scully settled into the patient silence of countless stakeouts. Scully sometimes thought stakeouts were the most difficult part of her job. It was so easy to get bored and distracted, to let your thoughts drift and stop paying attention . . .

Mulder tapped her on the arm, and she realized she'd done just that. He nodded toward the house, and she lifted the binoculars and scanned the front of the Reardon home. Cindy had appeared almost eerily in the upper-level window.

Curious, Scully adjusted the lens setting, trying to get a better view. She could see the girl's slim form, the outline of the bed. Then, behind Cindy, a blazing white light suddenly glared out from the closet as the folding doors were yanked open.

Scully dropped the binoculars as she saw

Cindy jerk away from the window, as if some-one had grabbed her from behind.

"Mulder, let's go!" Scully said, starting out of the car.

"I'll take the back!" Mulder shouted, sprinting toward the wooden fence that sur-rounded the yard.

Scully lost sight of her partner as she raced toward the front of the house.

She pounded on the door, waiting impa-tiently for Mrs. Reardon to open it.

It seemed ages before a bathrobe-clad Ellen Reardon came to the door.

"What is it?" the woman asked, sounding sleepy and disoriented.

"There's someone upstairs," Scully said, pushing past her. "Wait outside."

Silently Mulder let himself in through the red-wood gate that led into the Reardons' yard. He slowed as he approached the back of the house. There was no sign of a break-in. Then again, whoever had grabbed Cindy couldn't have come through the front. FBI agents had been watching the front of the house round-the-clock for the past forty-eight hours. Which meant that whoever they were up against was good at this game. Frighteningly good.

Mulder shined his flashlight in front of him and raised his gun.

Scully rushed up the darkened stairs, her weapon drawn. As she reached the landing at the top of the stairs, she raised the gun, cupping one hand beneath the other for support. Using the wall as cover, she spun into the upstairs hallway.

Nothing.

She moved quickly, silently, heading for Cindy's room. She hoped Mrs. Reardon had thought to call the police. Because Scully could feel someone else in the house with her. Someone who was very close . . .

Mulder scanned the shadows in the yard. Was whoever had grabbed Cindy still in the house?

And would they come out the back? His eyes fell on the swing, the place where Doug Reardon's body had been found. Another thought suddenly occurred to him: There was a good chance that whoever was after Cindy wasn't working alone. What if there was an accomplice hiding in the yard?

Silently Mulder began to edge his way around the garden fence.

From the darkened hall, a figure emerged behind Scully—and struck her hard on the head. Scully gave a cry and fell to the floor. Her assailant plowed over her, leaving her unconscious on the landing.

Scully had no awareness of the hooded figure who sprang over her and down the steps, carrying Cindy Reardon.

She never even heard Mrs. Reardon's horrified scream.

In the Reardons' backyard, Mulder whirled at the sound of the scream. Without warning, the patio's sliding glass door shattered into a million pieces. The abductor charged out, backward, protecting the girl.

Glass rained into the yard as Mulder pulled his weapon. "FBI! I'm armed!" he shouted.

The kidnapper swung the girl in front, using the child as a human shield.

Mulder held his gun steady, but he knew he couldn't risk advancing. He concentrated on the kidnapper, a figure dressed in black pants, black gloves, and a black hooded jacket, holding a very frightened Cindy Reardon captive. Doing the only thing he could, Mulder raised his flashlight.

And he saw the pale, familiar face of Sally Kendrick.

"Drop it," Kendrick ordered, resting the butt of her gun against Cindy's temple. "You know I'm capable."

Mulder stood frozen, wanting to stall her, willing to try anything.

"Which one are you?" he asked. "Eve Seven or Eve Eigh . . ."

The sound of the gun being cocked froze

the words in his throat. Sally Kendrick had won, for now. Mulder began to lower his weapon.

"Put it down slow," Kendrick told him. "Very slow."

Reluctantly Mulder set his weapon on the ground.

Still holding her gun on Cindy, Sally Kendrick edged out of the yard, then ran through the open back gate.

The second she was out of sight, Mulder picked up his gun and went after her. His heart sank as he reached the street and saw that Kendrick already had the girl in the backseat of a light blue Toyota sedan.

Kendrick must have heard him running. Reacting faster than he would have thought possible, she spun around, faced him, and fired.

Mulder hit the ground behind the gate as the bullet sped by. *Another piece of information about the Eves*, he thought: *They made excellent markswomen.*

Kendrick didn't wait to take a second shot.

She got into the car and tore out, tires squealing.

Mulder drew his gun as he heard the car screeching away. He was up and over the gate in seconds. He ran hard, his lungs burning as he chased the blue Toyota. But it did no good. Sally Kendrick and her victim were out of sight in seconds.

Chapter Twelve

In front of the Reardon house, red and blue lights strobed from an army of police cars. For the second time that week, neighbors thronged the street, held back by the police barricades, wondering what had befallen Ellen Reardon.

Scully walked up to a group of officers. They were gathered around a police car with a map of the bay area spread out across its hood.

"The suspect's name is Sally Kendrick," Scully said, briefing them. "Early forties. Five foot eight, a hundred and thirty-five pounds. She may have an accomplice, similar in appearance. Kendrick is driving a light blue '93 Corolla.

"She has exceptional strength for her size,"

Scully went on. "So you must consider her armed and dangerous. Quite possibly she'll display severe psychotic behavior."

Scully nodded to a couple of FBI agents waiting nearby. "The Oakland bureau is here to orchestrate the search across the bridge."

As the Oakland agents unfolded another map, Scully moved off in search of Mulder. She found her partner trying to comfort Mrs. Reardon.

"What if she . . . kills her?" Mrs. Reardon asked. "First I lose Doug. Now Cindy . . ."

"Mrs. Reardon, the fact that Kendrick and her accomplice murdered the fathers and abducted the girls tells us that they want the girls alive," Mulder assured her. "I'm sure Cindy is alive, and we'll find her."

The distraught mother turned away from him.

"We'll find her," he promised again.

Mrs. Reardon nodded, but tears were streaming down her cheeks.

Mulder's eyes met his partner's. Scully's expression was tense. She spoke softly so that

Mrs. Reardon wouldn't hear her, but her question was a hard one: "And then what do we do?" she asked.

Forty miles north of San Francisco, just off the San Andreas Fault, the waves of the Pacific swept in against the grass-covered bluffs of Point Reyes National Seashore. Just a few miles inland, at the Lighthouse Motel, the smell of salt water and the cries of the gulls still filled the air.

The woman who pulled up to the motel early the next morning hadn't chosen it for its atmosphere or even its closeness to the beach. The Lighthouse Motel was a long, white one-story building, surrounded by eucalyptus trees and redwoods. It was remote and quiet. Despite the NO VACANCY sign, there were no other cars around, which was exactly the way she wanted it.

She parked the dark blue Ford in front of her room and got out. In the morning light, her hair was redder and shorter than it had been in the Stapes Center video. Sally Kendrick was older now and her resemblance to Eve Six even stronger.

Nonchalantly she checked to see if anyone was watching. When she was satisfied they were alone, she opened the rear car door, removed Cindy Reardon from the backseat, and led her into the motel room.

Sally Kendrick never noticed the gray-haired motel manager raking the lawn. But he noticed her.

Kendrick nudged Cindy into the room, smiling encouragingly at the little girl. "I'm sorry you have to meet this way," she said. "But it's best for all concerned."

Cindy looked around wordlessly. The large room, which was both kitchen and living room, was decorated with flower-print curtains and a collection of cowboy hats hanging on the wall. An open door toward the back led into a bedroom.

Kendrick took off her gloves and peered out the kitchen window to make certain they hadn't been followed. Then she opened the bathroom door and pushed Cindy in ahead of her.

Inside the bathroom Teena Simmons sat tied on the toilet seat, a gag on her mouth, her arms bound behind her. She wore a red coat, red tights, a red plaid blouse, and a red skirt. She gazed in fascination at Cindy, who was still in her pajamas.

Kendrick untied the gag, then put an arm around her, saying, "Teena Simmons, meet Cindy Reardon."

For a long moment, the girls looked at each other, their expressions unreadable. And then, at the exact same moment, they smiled.

The Reardons' house had become the nerve center of the investigation. Police officers and lab experts swarmed through the rooms, checking for traces of the kidnapper. The home phones and portable ones were ringing off the hook. The energy in the house was charged. Time was of the essence, and everyone knew it.

A uniformed female officer, Sergeant Mann, hustled past the others, approaching the two FBI agents who were coming down the stairs. Mulder was talking on his cellular phone.

"Agents Scully, Mulder," Mann said breathlessly. "They found the light blue Corolla in the parking lot of San Francisco International Airport."

"Oh, good," Scully murmured. She looked at her partner, who was still on the phone, and knew she'd have to give the orders alone this time. "Okay," she said, thinking fast. "I want you to start a check on every single passenger list for every flight that left the terminal within the past twelve hours . . ."

Mulder finished his call, folded up the phone, then unfolded it as it rang yet again. "Mulder here . . ."

Scully continued giving instructions to the police officers. "I want you to check every single terminal and make sure Kendrick's not hiding out for a later flight. And remember, she may have an accomplice."

The officers began to move out as Mulder finished his call.

"That was a motel manager in Point Reyes," Mulder told his partner. "He's a cop wannabe. Heard the APB on a police scanner. Says he has a guest matching Kendrick's description."

"We just found the car *at the airport*," Scully said, dismissing the motel manager's call.

"She might have ditched it," Mulder pointed out.

Reluctantly Scully realized that Mulder could be right. Kendrick was certainly smart enough to switch cars. They couldn't afford to overlook any lead.

"The manager says this woman checked in with the little girl," Mulder went on. "And she leaves the motel in the afternoon *by herself*, is gone all night, and then returns *with the little girl*."

Scully had no trouble imagining a scenario that would account for this. "Someone could have picked up the girl without the manager knowing about it. I mean, that area is filled with vacationing families. There could be hundreds of little kids running around."

"In November?" Mulder asked skeptically. The Point Reyes area had beautiful summer weather, but it was also known for its cold, blustery winters. "Besides," Mulder went on, "the manager remembers this kid. She told him he should use chlorine to eradicate the dinoflagellates in the swimming pool. Does that sound like someone you know?"

"Let's go," Scully said with a sigh.

Chapter Thirteen

Teena Simmons and Cindy Reardon sat at opposite ends of the table in the kitchen area of the motel room. They were wearing identical red plaid blouses, red skirts, and red tights. Sally Kendrick had brought them take-out food for lunch, and now the table was covered with fast-food wrappers, cardboard containers, and plastic soft-drink cups.

"I've always kept a close eye on your behavior," Kendrick told them. "No matter where I was. The last few years I've spent in search of the remaining Eve," she explained. "That, however, was cut short by your . . . activity."

Kendrick sat down at the table with the two eight-year-olds and rested her head on her hands. "I had hoped my work at the

Stapes Center had corrected the Litchfield flaws," she said, addressing them as peers. There was no reason to talk down to them, and they needed to know about their own unusual heritage. "Psychotic behavior didn't develop in the Adams and Eves until age sixteen," she explained. "Homicidal behavior at twenty."

She started to gather up some of the empty wrappers on the table. "Imagine my . . . disappointment when I learned of your *accelerated* development."

The girls listened quietly, not reacting. As if they were deaf.

Kendrick got up and threw away the trash, grateful for the distraction. She returned to the table, wondering what to say next. She'd thought this would be easier. She knew they understood her. After all, genetically they were nearly identical to her and the other Eves. Possibly they were even more intelligent. Why was it so difficult to talk to them? She decided to try another tactic.

"How did you learn of each other's existence?" she asked curiously.

The two girls exchanged a glance and shrugged.

"We just knew," Teena said at last.

"Did you discuss how you would orchestrate your little . . . prank?" Kendrick found herself feeling surprisingly anxious. The girls' eerie calm—especially after being kidnapped—was unnerving.

"We just knew," Cindy said.

"Why murder your fathers?" Kendrick asked, her voice pained. Even she couldn't have predicted that one; she'd foolishly assumed that the girls wouldn't be a danger at least until their teens.

Again, the two girls just shrugged.

"They *weren't* our fathers," Cindy said at last.

"We have no parents," Teena chimed in.

"We weren't born," Cindy said.

"We were created," Teena said, her eyes angry and resentful.

"Y-You cannot think that way," Kendrick stammered. She certainly understood how they felt; and it was the last thing on earth she'd wanted. It was, in fact, exactly what she'd wanted to prevent.

"You're human beings," she said, speaking slowly and distinctly. "Different. Special. But you *cannot* give in to genetic destiny."

Kendrick swayed in her chair, suddenly feeling a little light-headed. She forced herself to continue.

"That's why I've taken you," she said desperately. "I was raised by a man who knew what I was. He was a genetic engineer on the project. You need to be with someone who understands your sp-special abilities."

Kendrick was having trouble speaking now. She felt nauseated and dizzy, and even though she was wearing a wool turtleneck, she was suddenly freezing cold. Her teeth were chattering uncontrollably. She forced herself to ignore all that, to tell the girls the things they had to understand.

"With a proper environment and a program

of long-term medication . . . you can become like me . . . and . . . not the other Eves . . ." She tried to smile encouragingly at the girls, but something was wrong. It was nearly impossible to talk. Her body was shaking violently.

The girls watched her dispassionately.

She got up from the table and made her way over to the sink. She gagged but couldn't throw up. She turned to the girls, apologetic.

And caught them grinning at each other.

Kendrick went white with horror. "Wh-What have you done?" she gasped.

"Your soda," Teena answered matter-of-factly. "Four ounces of digitalis."

"Extracted from a foxglove plant," Cindy added. She pulled a small glass vial from her pocket, then held her thumb and forefinger less than an inch apart. "This much is a lethal dose."

"We cultivated the plants ourselves," Teena said proudly. "The purple flowers were really pretty."

Kendrick grabbed the edge of the sink, trying to hold herself upright. She could feel the drug accelerating through her system, horror paralyzing her thoughts. She tried to turn to the girls, and her legs collapsed under her. She slid to the floor in front of the stove.

"W-Why?" she asked, terrified.

"You tell us," Cindy challenged her.

"You made us," Teena said accusingly.

"We're *your* mistake," Cindy reminded her coolly.

Kendrick knew what she had to do. She reached up behind her to the large kitchen knife she'd left on top of the stove. She forced herself to stand and walk toward them, her voice determined. "Then I'll correct that mistake."

Chapter Fourteen

It was a cool, overcast afternoon in Point Reyes, the kind of quiet day when the locals took solitary walks on the beach or long afternoon naps. But at the Lighthouse Motel police cars filled the parking lot, and the heavy static of their radios broke the day's stillness.

A local law enforcement officer stood waiting impatiently by his vehicle. He felt himself relax a little as he saw the two FBI agents arrive, escorted by another local police cruiser. He didn't really understand who was supposed to be hiding out here or why the FBI was so intent on taking care of this matter itself. He couldn't even remember the last time federal agents had shown up in Point Reyes.

The two agents got out of their car hurriedly. *Well, whatever it is*, the officer thought, *it must be important.*

"I waited, just like you told me," the officer said, walking up to Scully and Mulder. "No one's come in . . . or gone out, that I could tell—"

A scream burst out from one of the rooms, and a window shattered.

"Get back!" Mulder ordered. For an endless moment they all waited tensely. Then, at a nod from Mulder, the police officers started toward Sally Kendrick's room, with Mulder and Scully following close behind.

The officer in the lead didn't waste time knocking. He simply kicked the door down.

Scully and Mulder stepped into the room and gazed around in dismay. They were too late. The room was in shambles. Dishes and clothing were scattered everywhere.

And Sally Kendrick lay on her side, her eyes wide open, staring sightlessly. Blood oozed from her mouth and nose, soaking the carpet beneath her head.

Mulder stepped toward the body, his gun raised. He knelt beside Kendrick briefly and saw what he'd already guessed. She wasn't breathing.

Suspecting that Eve Eight might still be nearby, Mulder headed for the bedroom. It was even more chaotic than the kitchen area. The blankets and sheets looked as if they'd been ripped from the beds. The mirror on the wall hung at a strange angle. A shade was torn from the top of the window, and the window glass was smashed.

Mulder searched the room with his gun raised. There had definitely been some sort of struggle in here, he decided. And whoever had killed Sally Kendrick had obviously escaped through the back window.

In the main room, Scully knelt by Kendrick's body and placed two fingers on her throat just beneath her ear, even though she already knew there'd be no pulse.

Her gaze fell on the two girls, huddled against the wall, clutching each other for comfort. The girls were dressed identically in red: red plaid blouses, red skirts, red tights. In fact, Scully thought with a chill, they were dressed a lot like the young Eves in the photograph in Eve Six's cell.

Scully moved toward the two girls, wondering how to comfort them. They were so young, and they'd been through so much.

"We were all supposed to drink," Cindy explained clearly. "But we only pretended to drink it."

"They tried to poison us," Teena added solemnly.

Mulder walked in and glanced at the table. Two empty glasses stood there. Two others still had soda in them. Strange that in all this disarray, the cups remained untouched. Mulder made a mental note of it, and then turned his attention to Scully as she started to question the girls.

"Who's 'they'?" Scully asked.

Teena pointed to Sally Kendrick. "She and the other lady."

"What did the other lady look like?" Mulder asked.

Both girls pointed to Sally Kendrick.

"Eve Eight," Mulder said, unsurprised. "They were working together."

The two girls held on to each other and began to sob uncontrollably.

Scully knelt beside them, feeling helpless to comfort them. She stroked Teena's hair. "It's all right," she said gently.

"We'll take care of you. You're safe with us," she promised as the two young murderers continued to cry.

Chapter Fifteen

Dusk was settling over Point Reyes, and the parking lot of the Lighthouse Motel was still filled with police cars. Their blue and red lights flashed silently as another vehicle drove in: a coroner's van.

Inside the motel room, Marin County detectives were busy recording the crime scene. A woman officer dusted for prints while another took a series of photographs of the room and the body. A third officer was searching the outside of the motel for any sign of the escape vehicle.

Mulder and Scully examined the kitchen area for clues to what had happened. Reconstructing a murder was tricky, Mulder knew. Even with the strongest evidence, it was possible to misinterpret, to construct a scenario that had nothing to do with the actual crime. *We need witnesses,* he thought. *And we have them. The problem is, the witnesses are only eight years old and falling apart.*

Scully snapped on a pair of latex gloves and peered into one of the glasses on the table.

"Looks as if the Eves mixed about four ounces of digitalis in each glass," she said, examining the residue in the cup.

"Their own mini-Jonestown," Mulder remarked. In 1974 a San Francisco religious leader named Jim Jones established a commune near Georgetown, Guyana, which he named Jonestown. He not only persuaded many of his followers to move to Jonestown, but in 1978 he convinced them to commit mass suicide.

"Yeah, that was a weird one," one of the uniformed officers said. "Nine hundred and eleven people—over two hundred of 'em kids—thought they were following Jones to paradise and swallowed cyanide."

Scully shook her head. "Maybe a few really believed that and actually committed suicide, but . . ."

Mulder gave her one of his fleeting half smiles. "You think most of them were murdered."

Scully nodded. "I think most of them were forced to drink the poison. I can't believe over nine hundred people voluntarily committed suicide."

Mulder's eye returned to the white sheet covering Sally Kendrick's body. "Eve Six said the other Eves were prone to suicide." That, he somehow found very believable.

Scully sniffed at one of the glasses that still had cola in it. "No odor, but digitalis can have a sweet flavor," she said thoughtfully. "It's probably not even perceptible in soda."

A Marin County detective approached the two FBI agents. "We're still searching in the area, but so far, there's no sign of the other suspect. We'll have an officer take the girls back."

"No," Mulder said at once. "Maybe it would be best if we take responsibility for the girls." Mulder knew this was not standard procedure, but he was reluctant to let the girls out of his sight, and he certainly didn't want them to spend the night in some sort of institutional shelter. They'd been through enough.

"I'd like to get them checked out by a doctor," Scully said, backing him up.

"Okay, whatever," the detective agreed easily.

Satisfied that the police could handle the crime scene, Scully and Mulder got ready to leave. They found the two girls outside, where they were being watched by another police officer.

"Come on, girls, we'll take you back," Scully said.

"Back where?" Teena asked.

That's a good question, Scully thought.

"What's going to happen to Teena?" Cindy wanted to know.

"We'll talk about that in the car, okay?" Mulder said. He helped the two girls into the car, then shut the door.

Scully turned to him, concerned. "They've already grown so attached," she said. "It's going to be hard for them when Teena's placed in foster care."

"Yeah," Mulder agreed, wishing there were some way to keep the girls together.

When they were all buckled in, Mulder started driving, concentrating on the road. Scully, who was sitting beside him, turned back now and then to check on the girls. Cindy and Teena sat side by side, quiet and well behaved.

Mulder felt grateful that the girls weren't pressing him for an answer about Teena. She'd probably be returned to the hostel in Greenwich. He wondered idly if Mrs. Reardon would have any interest in adopting her—a second exceptional child.

In the back of the car, the girls remained silent. But every time Scully checked, they were holding hands and watching each other with a curious intensity.

Scully blinked as a strange and improbable thought came to her, a very Mulderesque thought: If she hadn't known how impossible it was, she'd have sworn the girls were communicating telepathically.

Chapter Sixteen

A thick fog had rolled in with the night. The headlights of the rental car shone through the darkness, reflecting on misty, white vapor. Figuring his visibility was about fifty feet, Mulder slowed the car. The road he was on was definitely the longer route into the city, but to Mulder it was worth it. He was wary of Eve Eight. He wouldn't put it past her to be somewhere on the main road, waiting to make another attempt on the girls' lives. And yet something about that scenario nagged at him: Why had the two Eves gone to the trouble of kidnapping the girls only to try to get them to commit suicide? Had the girls refused to do what the Eves wanted? He'd give a lot to know what had really happened in that motel room. Maybe later, he thought, the girls would open up and tell them.

He glanced in the back mirror. The two girls were still sitting silently, holding hands.

To his surprise, Cindy suddenly spoke up. "Agent Mulder, I have to go to the bathroom."

"Me too," Teena chimed in.

Scully eyed Mulder, amused.

"Can you hold it?" Mulder asked, wanting to get the girls to safety.

"I really need to go," Cindy insisted.

"I could use some caffeine," Scully said, clearly on the girls' side.

Mulder sighed, knowing he was outnumbered. A short time later he saw a truck stop at the side of the road. There was a fueling station for the trucks and, just beyond it, a diner, already lit with colored Christmas lights.

Mulder pulled off the road and parked near the restaurant. Outside, the night was damp and bone-chillingly cold. He pulled his coat close as he, Scully, and the two girls started toward the restaurant.

The inside of the diner was brightly lit and

inviting. Mulder eyed the sandwich menu, wishing they had enough time for the luxury of a real meal.

A young, dark-haired waitress in a pale yellow uniform passed him as she carried plates of food to a table. "Be with you in a sec," she called.

Mulder and Scully and the two girls walked up to the take-out counter, where they waited for her.

"Excuse me," Mulder said when the waitress finished with her table. "Where are the rest rooms?"

The waitress pointed across the restaurant, past two video game machines to a hallway. "In the back. But you'll need a key." She handed him two ridiculously large key rings, each attached to a thick rectangle of wood. *No one would accidentally walk off with these keys*, Mulder thought.

He gave Scully the women's room key, and she and the two girls started off. Mulder hung back. "Can I get four diet sodas?" he asked the waitress.

The two girls turned. "Regular!" Cindy and Teena insisted at once.

"All right," Mulder corrected himself, amused. "Two diet and two regular sodas, to go. Please."

Smiling, the waitress wrote down the order.

Mulder followed the girls down the hallway, past the video games. He went into the men's room while Scully and the two girls entered the women's room.

A few seconds later the door of the women's room cracked open and Cindy let herself back into the hall. Inside the women's room Teena's voice drifted over the top of the cubicle. "Agent Scully, my door is stuck."

"Just a second," Scully said.

Knowing that her twin would handle Scully, Cindy returned to the restaurant's take-out counter. Four sodas to go were sitting next to the cash register. Cindy's small hands stretched up, returned the rest room key, then grabbed two of the sodas.

"Hold on, just a minute . . ." the waitress said.

Cindy turned to face her. "It's okay," she

said calmly. "My dad'll pay for them when he gets out of the bathroom."

Surprised by the child's self-possession, the waitress smiled and nodded, giving Cindy permission to take the drinks.

Cindy moved to a nearby booth with the sodas. Carefully she looked around her. Then she produced a glass vial from her pocket, lifted the plastic lids on the cups—and added a lethal dose of digitalis to each.

Very gently Cindy began to stir the drinks. She had just put the lids back on when she saw Mulder approaching.

"Those are the diet?" he asked, joining her at the table.

"I think these are," Cindy said, offering him a poisoned soda.

Mulder dropped his keys onto the table and took a sip through the straw. "Are you sure?" he asked. "It's really sweet. Try it."

Cindy tensed and edged back a little. "I-I know it's diet," she insisted. "I saw the waitress pour it."

"Okay," Mulder said with a smile. He liked

the twins and their quiet self-assurance. Despite the bizarre circumstances of their birth and the past few weeks, they showed every sign that they'd grow up to be smart, interesting adults.

Scully returned from the women's room with Teena beside her. "Let's go," she said.

"C'mon," Mulder said to Cindy. The two of them had started for the door when Teena said, "Don't forget the drinks!"

Mulder and Cindy quickly turned and walked back to the take-out counter while Scully and Teena waited.

"How much?" Mulder asked the waitress, a little embarrassed that he'd forgotten to pay.

The waitress checked the bill. "Five dollars," she replied.

"Want to pay?" Mulder asked Cindy, offering her the money.

"Sure," Cindy said, smiling.

Cindy paid and took the two untainted drinks. She handed one to Teena.

"Thanks," Mulder said to the waitress while he handed Scully a poisoned diet soda.

Chapter Seventeen

Scully walked out of the restaurant, holding on to Teena with one hand and holding her soda with the other. Beside her, Teena looked straight ahead. Their breath turned to white vapor in the chill night air.

Scully sipped from her drink as they started down the steps of the restaurant. "Hmm . . . tastes syrupy," she said.

At those words Teena turned around. Behind her, Cindy, who was walking beside Mulder, was smiling. Their plan was working.

The agents and the girls crossed the parking lot to the rental car. Mulder set his soda on its hood as he reached into the pocket of his coat. He grimaced as he realized his pockets were empty. "Cindy, you didn't pick up my keys from the counter, did you?" he asked.

"No," Cindy assured him.

"All right, I'll be right back." He began jogging back to the restaurant, annoyed with himself. First he'd forgotten the sodas, now the keys. Either he was exhausted or he was losing his mind. This should have been a five-minute stop. Somehow it felt more like thirty.

Outside, standing beside the car, the two girls watched intently as Scully raised the straw to her lips and took another sip of her soda.

Inside the diner Mulder started toward the booth where Cindy had been waiting for him. He was aware of the waitress cleaning off tables and hoped she hadn't gotten to that one yet. It'd just be too embarrassing to have to admit that he'd not only forgotten to pay, but then he'd forgotten his keys. *Agents with Alzheimer's,* he thought despairingly.

He reached the booth, relieved to see that the table was untouched. His keys were still there. He reached for them and then stopped.

No, he thought, *it couldn't be*. But he bent forward and took a closer look.

The edge of the table was lightly dusted with a dark green powder. Curious, Mulder touched it with his forefinger, then touched his finger to his tongue. It was almost as if he'd touched it with Novocain. The spot where the powder touched his tongue went completely numb.

Mulder felt himself go hollow with shock as the pieces of the puzzle finally fell into place. It had all been so clear. He'd simply refused to see the obvious. Now he finally understood how Joel Simmons, Doug Reardon, and Sally Kendrick had died.

And Mulder knew he didn't have another second to waste.

He took off, bursting out of the restaurant, sprinting toward the car.

"Scully!" Mulder shouted as he raced down the stairs and across the parking lot.

"What?" Scully said, taking another sip of her soda.

Mulder was about to shout a warning, but

he had second thoughts as he saw the two girls.

Cindy and Teena waited by the rear driver's side door. They watched Mulder running across the parking lot, their expressions suspicious.

Forcing himself to play it cool, Mulder slowed and walked toward Scully. "Just wanted to unlock the car door for you," he said, smiling.

Scully looked at him as if he'd just lost his mind, but she didn't say anything. After all, Mulder had certainly done stranger things in the time they'd worked together.

Mulder moved to open her door and knocked the soda from her hand, making it appear as if he'd just been clumsy.

"Mulder!" Scully said, sounding annoyed.

"Oh, I'm sorry," Mulder apologized, then added under his breath, "It's them. They poisoned it. Let's just try to get them in the car."

"Okay," Scully said at once. Scully had learned to trust her partner, no matter how far out his theories seemed. And actually, for a while now, she'd been having nagging doubts about the Eve Eight theory.

Determined to act perfectly normal, Scully refrained from looking at the girls.

But Mulder looked where they'd been standing—and saw only two sodas resting on the ground.

Teena and Cindy were gone, hidden somewhere in the fogbound night.

Chapter Eighteen

Mulder stared at the two soda cups on the ground. The girls had been standing there a second before, and now they were gone. For a wild second he wondered if vanishing into thin air was one of their unusual genetic abilities.

He checked on the other side of the car, calling their names. How could they have just disappeared?

"Teena, Cindy," he called again.

"They're gone," Scully said.

Mulder turned to his partner, realizing they might have another problem. "We both drank the poison," he said.

"How much did you have?" Scully asked at once.

"I only had a sip."

"We probably haven't ingested enough to get sick," she said.

"Let's hope not," Mulder said, scanning the area for possible hiding places.

The restaurant's parking lot was filled with trucks. Row after row of tractor-trailers and eighteen-wheelers threw long, rectangular shadows across the ground. Strips of reflectors outlined their doors and taillights, glowing red in the darkness.

Mulder and Scully began to comb the lot. Scully's eyes scanned the trucks, dismayed by how many different kinds there were: transport for heavy machinery, farm produce, furniture, car and computer parts. There was even an oil tanker. Of course, each truck had a slightly different shape. Some had ladders that went up to their roofs; others had platforms underneath their carriage. Every one, she thought worriedly, provided dozens of hiding places. The girls weren't very big. They didn't need a fancy hiding place. All they had to do was crouch down behind one of the huge tires and no one would ever see them.

Determined not to miss anything, she methodically began walking the aisles of trucks and semis. The parking lot smelled of oil, gas, and exhaust fumes. At least no one had pulled out of the lot, she reminded herself. The girls had to be here somewhere.

Mulder was working on another section of the vast lot. It had rained recently. An oil-streaked puddle reflected his own worried expression. He crouched down, checking beneath the trucks, wondering just how much chance they had of finding two eight-year-old geniuses with a definite criminal bent.

It was amazing, he thought, how quickly his perception of the girls had changed. Ten minutes ago, he'd felt sorry for them. Now he considered them as dangerous as any criminal he'd ever stalked. Maybe more so, because no one else would believe that they'd already murdered their fathers—and Sally Kendrick.

He should have seen through their act, Mulder thought angrily. How could he have let himself be fooled by them?

Mulder stopped and looked around the lot.

There was no sound, no sign of movement . . . except in the aisle ahead of him. For a split second, he saw the cables beneath a truck jiggle. He saw Scully at the other end of the row, also watching the cables.

Suddenly the two girls appeared. They sprinted across the aisle and disappeared behind another row of parked trucks. Scully and Mulder split up in pursuit.

Mulder peered beneath trucks, looking for footprints in the oil slicks under the vehicles.

Scully, her gun raised, listened for the slightest noise. Her heart sank as she found a truck whose open trailer was loaded with huge steel pipes. The girls could fit in any one of these, she realized. Patiently she began to peer inside each of the pipes. Empty. Empty. Empty. She checked beneath the truck, her flashlight illuminating the platform that held the truck's spare tires. Nothing there, either.

Mulder's pulse quickened as he saw Teena and Cindy scoot beneath one of the parked trucks and come out on the other side. As they neared the front of the row, Mulder appeared from behind. With a lightning-quick movement, he grabbed the two girls by the backs of their jackets.

The girls began to struggle wildly. Mulder thought of what Eve Six had said. He'd already had proof that the girls had heightened intelligence and psychosis. Now he had no doubt that they also had extraordinary strength. Trying to hold on to them was like trying to hold on to two young mountain lions.

"Scully, I've got them!" he shouted, desperate for backup.

But the girls were screaming, too. "Help! Leave us alone! He's hurting us!"

As Mulder held the struggling twins, the driver of a nearby truck heard the commotion. He peered into his side mirror and saw a man in a long, dark coat holding two obviously terrified little girls.

"Hey!" he shouted.

Mulder struggled to hold on to the girls as the door to the truck was flung open and a short, barrel-chested man wearing a plaid flannel shirt strode toward him. A tall woman in jeans and a camouflage vest followed close behind. The man was carrying a shotgun, the woman a crowbar. She looked a bit apprehensive, Mulder thought, but the man was more than ready for a fight. *Terrific*, Mulder thought. *Just what I need—truckers to the rescue.*

The man aimed the shotgun at Mulder.

"What the hell do you think you're doing?" he demanded in a threatening tone.

"Help!" Teena shrieked. "He's beating us!"

"He's trying to hurt us!" Cindy wailed, her voice even more hysterical.

"Back off," Mulder commanded. "I'm a federal agent."

"And these two are 'America's Most Wanted'?" the man asked skeptically.

Scully arrived on the scene, but as she reached for her badge, the man turned his gun on her. "Hands in front," he ordered. "Let the girls go."

Scully raised her hands, knowing better than to argue with a shotgun.

As the trucker trained his gun on her, the

girls twisted out of Mulder's grasp.

"Get in the truck, girls!" the woman urged them. "Get in!"

The girls scrambled toward the cab's open door.

"I'm calling the police," the woman warned the agents.

"*We are the police!*" Scully shouted. But it was too late. The girls were gone once again. "Mulder!" she called.

Mulder took off after the girls.

Flashing her FBI identification at the truckers, Scully raced after her partner.

On the other side of the parking lot, a yellow school bus pulled out from in front of the restaurant, its headlights reflecting the mist.

Mulder thought he saw the girls on the other side of the bus. "That way," he called, pointing toward the diner.

The two agents quickly entered the restaurant and immediately split up. Mulder ran toward the back of the diner while Scully approached the waitress.

"Have you seen the twins we were with?"

she called, holding up her ID.

"No—I . . ." the waitress answered, looking startled. She paused, then added, "There's a bunch of schoolkids that just left on that bus."

Mulder and Scully glanced out the window, then raced from the restaurant. Seconds later their rental car tore out of the parking lot and disappeared down the road in pursuit of the yellow school bus.

In another corner of the lot, someone had parked a station wagon that was towing a motorboat. It was only when the agents' car disappeared that the tarp covering the boat crinkled and then lifted.

Calmly Teena swung one leg over the side of the boat and jumped down. Once on the ground, she reached up to help Cindy down. The two girls looked quite pleased with themselves. They didn't bother to talk about what they would do next. As if they'd already agreed on a plan, they started out of the parking lot.

And that was when Mulder stepped up and grabbed them from behind.

"Forget your sodas, girls?" he asked sarcastically.

"We didn't do anything wrong," Teena said in an innocent voice.

"We're just little girls," Cindy assured him with a sweet smile.

"That's the *last* thing you are," Mulder said.

Chapter Nineteen

In the living room of the Reardon home, Mrs. Reardon stared at the framed photograph on the fireplace mantel. It had been her favorite picture of Cindy and her dad. Doug Reardon had been a handsome man with sandy hair, a blond mustache, and warm hazel eyes. In the photograph he was smiling, his arm around his daughter, the fall trees blazing brightly behind them.

"I took this picture just a year ago," Mrs. Reardon told the two agents, her voice strained but controlled. She was wearing a brown sweater over a blue blouse, its high collar closed with a silver pin. Scully didn't believe in judging a person by her clothes. But to her, the tightly pinned blouse seemed to mirror the woman's expression; something deep inside Ellen Reardon was closed, deliberately shut forever.

Scully studied the photograph thoughtfully. Cindy was staring straight into the camera with what Scully now saw as a calculating, disturbing look. The picture had been on the mantel the first time she and Mulder were in the house. But neither of them had picked up on the girl's true nature then. Neither of them had had a clue.

"They said they have an excellent program that can help . . . her," Mrs. Reardon went on, her voice trembling.

Mulder stepped forward, feeling tremendous sympathy for the woman. He wasn't about to tell her what kind of program probably awaited Cindy. In less than a week's time Ellen Reardon had lost her husband and the child she'd believed to be her daughter for the past eight years. Even worse, she'd discovered that her daughter had murdered her own father. And all of it had happened because nearly fifty years ago the U.S. government thought it had the right to interfere with human genetics.

"They can't hide behind a bureaucracy, Mrs. Reardon," Mulder told her. "You have every right to know what happened. You have a right to know about your daughter."

Mrs. Reardon took the photograph down from the mantel. "All I need to know is . . . she was *not* my daughter." The harsh words cut through the room like a knife. Her next words were so soft that Mulder barely heard them. "She never was."

Mrs. Reardon slid the photograph out of the frame and carefully tore it in half. Then she took the half with Cindy's picture and deliberately fed it to the flames. As Mulder and Scully watched, the picture of the smiling little girl curled and caught fire.

Mulder stared out the car window while Scully drove to San Francisco International Airport. Tonight they'd be back in Washington. Tomorrow they'd start on a new case. This one, though, would be hard to forget.

"Thinking about the girls?" Scully asked, slowing as she exited into the lanes leading to the Golden Gate Bridge. They hadn't even reached the city, and already traffic was crawling.

"And Eve Six and Mrs. Reardon. You know, we don't have any idea if any of the Adams are still alive."

Scully inched patiently toward the bridge. "I keep wondering what's going to happen to Teena and Cindy."

"There'll be a battery of tests done on them," Mulder predicted wearily. "Medical workups, IQ tests, ongoing psych studies. Every one of their actions will be monitored for the rest of their lives. Ultimately, they won't turn out too differently from the other Eves."

"They committed three murders," Scully reminded him. "It would have been five if we'd drunk those sodas."

Mulder nodded. "They're psychopaths, genetic mutants predisposed to murder. And what all the scientific studies on them are going to conclude is that our behavior is hard-wired into our genes. That all of us are genetically programmed to be a certain kind of person, act a certain way, even to experience certain kinds of moods. They're going to use the girls to try to prove that biology determines our fate and in the end nothing else matters."

"That's the old question of nature versus nurture," Scully said. "If you believe that genetics controls our destiny, then you leave no room for someone to be influenced by their family, their upbringing, or their own experiences. You rule out free will."

"How much free will did Teena and Cindy have?" Mulder asked bleakly. "They both grew up in loving households. A lot of good it did them." He frowned at the endless line of cars arcing across the bridge. "We'd make better time walking across."

"We have plenty of time to get to the airport," Scully said, refusing to give in to her partner's pessimism. "Besides, you've got to admit, it's a very scenic place to be stuck in traffic."

Mulder glared at her attempt at humor, so she returned to the real subject of their conversation. "Teena and Cindy and the Eves are all very extreme cases," Scully pointed out. "Some genetic conditions are so overwhelming that they control us. Obviously, a child born with Down's syndrome has serious limitations on what it can and can't do and definite tendencies toward certain types of behavior. But I believe most of us have more choice than that."

Mulder pulled a handful of sunflower seeds from his pocket. "I used to think so."

"You know," Scully went on thoughtfully as the San Francisco end of the bridge came into sight, "the good thing about all this research into genetics is that once a biological cause for a problem is identified, the problem can often be treated chemically. I mean, researchers have found that manic depression is linked to a genetic mutation, and they've been able to treat it successfully with drugs. Maybe they'll find something to help Teena and Cindy."

Typical, Mulder thought, *that Scully would*

take the optimistic view of genetic medicine. She was a scientist through and through. And certainly, he couldn't argue against effective treatments for devastating diseases. But somewhere deep inside, Mulder couldn't help wondering if human beings had *the right* to alter something as basic and profound as another person's genetic code. To Mulder, it was sheer arrogance to believe that because we have the ability to alter life, we also have the wisdom to understand all the consequences of that act. Even Sally Kendrick could not have predicted that Cindy and Teena would turn out the way they did.

"Tell me something, Scully," he said. "All this messing around with people's DNA—do you think it's right?"

"I think it's inevitable," Scully replied. "Right now our government is sponsoring a three-billion-dollar international Human Genome Project. Laboratories around the world are sending genetic codes, stored on disks, to genomic libraries. It's the next big thing in biotechnology. Everyone expects that breaking the genetic code will radically change twenty-first-century medicine. Doctors will be able to screen for thousands of disease-causing genes. That means diagnosing— and curing—most diseases before they ever start."

"I guess that's good, then," Mulder said.

Scully sent him an amused glance. "I don't think we can call it either good or bad. Like many things our species creates, genetic research has the potential to be used for good or to cause great harm."

She turned a question on him. "Don't you think there must be something in our species' genetic code that causes us to keep experimenting—to make bombs and spaceships, to play with genetics and gravity . . . and gourmet cooking?"

Mulder shifted in his seat as the traffic eased and they merged into the highway that led to the airport. This time he was the one who looked amused. "Maybe it's just that we can, Scully," he said. "The human animal has the ability to imagine these things and then find ways to make them real. And once we have that ability to try something new—whether it's creating computers or rearranging DNA—no matter how it alters life for future generations, you can bet that we'll use it."

Chapter Twenty

In the basement of the Whiting Institute for the Criminally Insane, well away from the other inmates, a narrow window slot slid open in the heavy steel door. The slot was reinforced with steel wire and only a few inches high—just high enough for the cell's inmate to look through it. Above the tiny window, the name on the door was EVE 6.

Eve Six peered out from the darkness of her cell, looking strangely pleased.

"Hello, girls," she said in her eerie, trembling voice.

She was looking at two doors directly across from her cell. One was labeled EVE 9, the other, EVE 10.

In the other cells, Teena Simmons and Cindy Reardon stepped up to the bars. Neither girl looked frightened. They studied Eve Six with calm, curious eyes and then smiled.

Eve Six returned their smiles. "So nice to have company," she said.

Upstairs a woman in a white lab coat strode toward the guard's desk in Cellblock Z. As she had dozens of times before, she presented her ID to the man in uniform.

The guard checked her credentials, then nodded. "Sign for this," he said, then issued her the same sort of panic-button beeper he'd given to Scully and Mulder.

The woman doctor nodded, then waited until another guard opened the first of the heavy steel doors. Without a word she turned and started down the stairs, not needing to be shown the way.

In the basement of Cellblock Z two pairs of eight-year-old eyes peered out from behind the heavy doors. They watched as a guard opened the final set of bars that cut their cells off from the others.

A woman in a white lab coat thanked the guard, then approached their cells. Cindy watched her, noting the differences. She had a small scar on one cheek. She wore her reddish brown hair pulled back neatly in a clip at the nape of her neck, and she wore tiny gold earrings. But those were minor things, differences that didn't really matter. The doctor was the exact image of Sally Kendrick.

"Hello, Eve Eight," Cindy said calmly.

"We've been waiting," Teena said.

"How did you know I'd come for you?" the doctor asked with a sly smile.

"We just knew," Cindy said.

"We just knew," Teena echoed.